HI! FLY GUY

Tedd Arnold

Cartwheel
·B·O·O·K·S·®
SCHOLASTIC INC.
New York   Toronto   London   Auckland
Sydney   Mexico City   New Delhi   Hong Kong

For Sam and Eli
—T.A.

Library of Congress Cataloging-in-Publication Data:

Arnold, Tedd.
Hi, Fly Guy! / by Tedd Arnold.
p. cm.
"Cartwheel books."
Summary: When Buzz captures a fly to enter in The Amazing Pet Show, his parents
and the judges tell him that a fly cannot be a pet, but Fly Guy proves them wrong.
ISBN 978-0-439-63903-3
[1. Flies—Fiction. 2. Pet shows—Fiction.] I. Title.

PZ7.A7379Hi 2005

[E]—dc22   2004020553

ISBN 978-0-439-63903-3

20 19 18   12 13 14

Printed in Singapore 46
First printing, September 2005

Chapter 1

A fly went flying.

He was looking
for something to eat—

something tasty,

something slimy.

A boy went walking.

He was looking for
something to catch—
something smart,
something for
The Amazing Pet Show.

They met.

The boy caught the
fly in a jar.
"A pet!" he said.

The fly was mad.
He wanted to be free.
He stomped his foot
and said— **BUZZ!**

The boy was surprised.
He said, "You know my name!
You are the smartest pet in
the world!"

Chapter 2

Buzz took the fly home.

"This is my pet," Buzz said to Mom and Dad.

"He is smart. He can say
my name. Listen!"

Buzz opened the jar.
The fly flew out.

"Flies can't be pets!" said
Dad. "They are pests!"
He got the fly swatter.
The fly cried— BUZZ!

And Buzz came to the rescue.
"You are right," said Dad.
"This fly _is_ smart!"

"He needs a name," said Mom.
Buzz thought for a minute.
"Fly Guy," said Buzz.
And Fly Guy said— BUZZ!

It was time for lunch.
Buzz gave Fly Guy
something to eat.

Fly Guy was happy.

Chapter 3

Buzz took Fly Guy to
The Amazing Pet Show.

The judges laughed.

"Flies can't be pets," they said.

"Flies are pests!"

Buzz was sad.

He opened the jar.

"Shoo, Fly Guy," he said.

"Flies can't be pets."

But Fly Guy liked Buzz.
He had an idea.
He did some fancy flying.

The judges were amazed.
"The fly can do tricks," they said.
"But flies can't be pets."

Then Fly Guy said—

The judges were more amazed. "The fly knows the boy's name," they said. "But flies can't be pets."

Fly Guy flew high, high, high
into the sky!

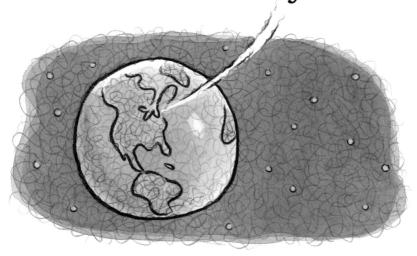

Then he dived down, down,
down into the jar.

"The fly knows his jar!" the judges said. "This fly _is_ a pet!" They let Fly Guy in the show.

He even won an award.

And *so* began a beautiful
friendship.